NUNA
GETS A CHANCE

by Monty Roberts
illustrated by Necdet Yilmaz

Harcourt
SCHOOL PUBLISHERS

Printed in China

ISBN 10: 0-15-350455-2
ISBN 13: 978-0-15-350455-6

Ordering Options
ISBN 10: 0-15-350333-5 (Grade 3 Below-Level Collection)
ISBN 13: 978-0-15-350333-7 (Grade 3 Below-Level Collection)
ISBN 10: 0-15-357467-4 (package of 5)
ISBN 13: 978-0-15-357467-2 (package of 5)

3 4 5 6 7 8 9 10 985 12 11 10 09 08

Nuna dashed into the house. "I am the
fastest girl in the world!" she announced.

Her mother frowned at her.

"Nuna, you're a mess!" she cried.
"Look at your sandals. They were new.
Now they already look old and shabby."

"I'm sorry, Mama," said Nuna.

Mama smiled. "Just try to be more careful. Inti is waiting to deliver a message. Now please help with dinner."

"May I go see Inti first?" begged Nuna.

Mama sighed. "Go. Hurry back, though. Clean up, too. You don't want to embarrass Inti."

Nuna's brother, Inti, was a *chasqui*, or messenger. *Chasquis* waited at posts. A message arrived. A *chasqui* raced with it to the next post. Then a new runner took over. Messages traveled quickly that way. *Chasquis* helped keep the big Inca nation together.

Nuna found Inti. He had a message. "Inti!"
Nuna shouted. "Let me run with you."

"Only a little," Inti said.

They took off.

"I ran up the hill today," Nuna panted.

He smiled. "That is good. Maybe some
day you will be a *chasqui*."

"I could be one now," Nuna said.

Suddenly, Inti fell! Nuna bent down. Inti had a dazed look on his face.

"It's my ankle," he groaned.

Nuna helped Inti back to the post. Inti handed Nuna a string with knots. It was a *quipu*. The knots were a code. They were the message.

"Find Atik," said Inti. "He will carry the message. Hurry. It's important."

Nuna searched. She couldn't find Atik.

"I am fast," Nuna thought. "Why not me?"

Nuna ran. The road was easy to follow. She wondered how far she would have to go.

Suddenly, the road came to an end. In front of Nuna was a stream with piles of rocks in it. The rocks elevated a plank above the water.

Nuna looked at the footbridge. "What if it collapses?" she thought. She had to get across. Inti said the message was important.

She took a deep breath. Then she stepped onto the plank. She took small steps. The bridge shook a little. At last, she made it across.

Nuna gladly raced up the road. She began to feel tired. Her legs felt heavy. Breathing was harder.

"Where is the next post?" she thought. "Is it far away?"

The road was long. Finally, she saw something. It was not a *chasqui* post. Instead, she saw a city. Nuna stared at the stone buildings. She was in Cuzco, the biggest Inca city.

Nuna ran into the city. She found a soldier in the midst of a crowd.

"I am a *chasqui*," she said. "I have a message."

He laughed. "You are not a *chasqui*. You are a child."

"Please," she begged. "It is important. Look." She held out the *quipu*.

The soldier looked at it. Then he led her to a building. Nuna waited outside.

A man came out. His clothes were fine. He wore gold.

"It is Sapa Inca," whispered the soldier. "Bow!"

Nuna fell to her knees. Sapa Inca was the ruler of all the Incas.

"Your message is important, *chasqui*," Sapa Inca said.

"My brother is the *chasqui*," Nuna said. "He is hurt. I am helping him."

Sapa Inca smiled. "Today, *you* are the *chasqui*. Good-bye, and thank you."

Nuna smiled. Then she headed home.

"Today, *I* am the *chasqui*!" she thought happily.

Think Critically

1. What does a *chasqui* do?

2. Is Nuna's statement about being "the fastest girl in the world" a fact or an opinion? Why?

3. What problem does Nuna solve?

4. How did Nuna's sandals get shabby so quickly?

5. Would you like to be a *chasqui*? Why or why not?

 Social Studies

Write a Paragraph Find out more about the Inca Empire. Where was it? When did the Incas live? Write a paragraph about the Incas.

 School-Home Connection Names often have meanings. *Nuna* means "spirit." *Inti* means "sun." Ask your family whether your name has a meaning.